W9-BUH-701

SECRET MISSION #4:
ROBOT RAMPAGE

BY GREG FARSHTEY

SCHOLASTIC INC.

No part of this publication may be reproduced, stored in a retrieval system, or transmitted in any form or by any means, electronic, mechanical, photocopying, recording, or otherwise, without written permission of the publisher. For information regarding permission, write to Scholastic Inc., Attention: Permissions Department, 557 Broadway, New York, NY 10012.

ISBN 978-0-545-47672-0

LEGO and the LEGO logo are trademarks of the LEGO Group. © 2013 The LEGO Group. Produced by Scholastic Inc. under license from the LEGO Group.

Published by Scholastic Inc. SCHOLASTIC and associated logos are trademarks and/or registered trademarks of Scholastic Inc.

12 11 10 9 8 7 6 5 4 3 2 1   13 14 15 16 17/0

Printed in the U.S.A.   40

First printing, February 2013

Prologue

Stringer ran for his life.

There was no other choice. This mission had gone bad in a hurry and now the only hope was escape. The question remaining was . . . escape to where?

It wasn't going to be back to Hero Factory, not anytime soon. His Hero craft was in ruins a little over a mile away. Every other ship capable of space travel was either smashed or too heavily guarded to do him any good. And he couldn't turn to the local authorities for help, because they were out to get him, too.

Next time, I'll ask Stormer for an easier job,

thought Stringer, *like exploring a supernova from the inside.*

His goal was in sight now. There was one communications tower still relatively undamaged in the city. If it still had power, he could get a message out to Hero Factory. Maybe they could send a rescue team.

Stringer was only two blocks away from his target. There was no one that he could see between him and the tower. But there were plenty of alleyways and other places for the enemy to hide. He had learned to be careful in his time on this planet.

He crouched down and listened, but heard nothing. The enemy had gotten craftier since he'd arrived. Stringer wondered if his skills at evasion had led to them improving their game.

Satisfied that now was his best chance, the Hero broke into a dead run, heading for the communications tower. Vaulting over rubble, dodging the spray of broken hydrants, and using wrecked vehicles as springboards, Stringer made it to within a few hundred yards of his destination.

If they're going to make a move, it's going to be now, he reasoned. *I wish I could make it harder for them.*

He glanced up, looking for anything that might help him bridge the distance between himself and where he needed to go. He spotted a flagpole still intact on the side of a building. Calculating the distance between it and the second-story window on the tower, Stringer had his plan.

Taking a running jump, the Hero grabbed on to the flagpole. Spinning around it until he had gained enough centrifugal force, Stringer suddenly let go and went sailing toward the window. He crashed through it, landing on his feet in an empty office.

Again, he paused, listening for sounds of movement. There were none. For a moment, he allowed himself to hope that the enemy had not made it here yet, though he dismissed the possibility that there might be survivors hiding in the building somewhere. His foe was nothing if not thorough.

I'm it, he thought. *Right now, I'm the only hope for every robot on this world. So I better not screw up.*

Stringer opened the door and scanned the empty hallway. Then he bolted from the office and made for the stairs. The main communications center would be on the top floor.

He took the steps three at a time. The metal door at the top of the staircase was locked, but a wave of sound from his sonic blaster blew it open. A solid kick was enough to bring down the door to the communications center.

Stringer hurried to the console. It was still turned on and there was still power flowing to it. He couldn't believe his luck.

After dialing to the correct frequency, Stringer grabbed the microphone and said, "Stringer to Hero Factory! Come in!"

There was a burst of static. Then Furno's voice came back, saying, "Stringer! Thank the stars! Are you all right?"

"No, Furno," Stringer replied. "I need transport off-world, now, and then we need to throw a quarantine around this place. I don't—"

From the corner of his optic sensor, Stringer saw something springing at him. By the time he could react, it was too late.

On the other end of the subspace radio, Furno heard a strangled cry. Then everything went dead. The fiery Hero slammed an alarm button.

"Red alert! Red alert!" Furno shouted into the comm system. "We've got a Hero in trouble!"

Furno, Bulk, and Stormer were assembled in the briefing room. The mood was tense. Furno, in particular, was having a hard time sitting still.

"We need to get going!" he said. "What are we waiting for?"

"A plan," said Bulk. "So sit down and pay attention."

Stormer called up a photo of a planet. "This is Tranquis VII. A week ago, all communications from the planet went silent. When we were unable to raise anyone on emergency frequencies, I dispatched Stringer to investigate."

"Right," said Bulk. "He called in when he got

there, but we haven't heard from him since . . . until today."

"When he called for *help*," Furno reminded the others, "which we aren't giving him by sitting around here doing nothing."

"Listen and learn, kid. Rocka did some checking on the message you got. It came in our frequency, but not from a Hero Factory comm system. So he wasn't calling from his ship."

"So what?" said Furno.

"So this," said Stormer. "Triangulating his signal, we found it came from a working communications tower in the capital city. If there was a working tower, why did the planet go silent?"

Furno shrugged. "Maybe there was a plague or a natural disaster, and there was nobody to operate the tower?"

"Could be," said Stormer. "Or maybe it was broken and just got repaired."

"You're leaving one out," Bulk said.

"What's that?" asked Furno.

"It *wasn't* working — and then it *was* — as bait for Stringer," said Bulk.

There were a few moments of grim silence. Then Stormer said, "All right, let's not get too far ahead of ourselves. Bulk, you and Furno take a Hero craft. Go find Stringer and bring him back."

Bulk stood up. "Got it. Let's go, kid."

Furno was already out the door.

By the time Bulk reached the hangar, Furno was already seated in the Hero craft's pilot seat, running instrument checks. Bulk immediately began shaking his head.

"Oh no," he said. "If we're flying, I'm driving."

"Bulk, listen—"

"The last time I let you pilot, the Hero craft wound up scattered all over the planetside," said Bulk. "You and your triple-spin-roll . . . my circuits ended up wrapped in knots around each other—so out of that chair!"

Reluctantly, Furno moved over. Bulk got behind the controls and immediately flipped open a small compartment on the main console.

"What's that?" asked Furno, leaning forward to get a better view.

"New feature," answered Bulk. "It's a chameleon screen. Makes the ship look like a cargo vessel instead of a Hero craft. You never know, we might not be popular on that planet. This new ship has everything, even an electromagnetic pulse emitter — shuts down anything mechanical that gets in our way."

"So this isn't going to be a 'pound on the front door' kind of mission?" said Furno as the hangar bay doors slowly slid open.

"Nah," said Bulk. "This is going to be 'sneak in the back window, get in, and get out' . . . If we're there more than a couple hours, we're doing something wrong."

Bulk hit the thruster. The ship rocketed out of Hero Factory and up into the atmosphere. In mere moments, the two Heroes were in space and headed for Stringer's last known position.

Bulk and Furno had been flying for most of the day, largely in silence. Furno, worried about Stringer, wasn't in the mood to chat. Finally, Bulk got tired of the silence.

"What's on your mind, Furno?"

Furno shrugged. "It's . . . this job. We get thrown into situations without having any idea what we're walking into. Last week, it was Rocka and Breez who almost didn't come back from a mission . . . now it's Stringer."

"So you want to quit?" asked Bulk, already knowing the answer.

"No. But maybe it would be smarter, and safer, for Hero Factory to act, instead of react: If we think there's a trouble spot, we strike first, instead of waiting to be attacked. Maybe things wouldn't get so out of hand then . . . and maybe Stringer wouldn't be in whatever danger he's in."

Bulk nodded and was quiet for a few moments. Then he said, "That came up once before. But one Hero argued against it. He said we would be setting ourselves up as judge and jury for the galaxy. Instead of being respected, we'd wind up being feared. That would be the beginning of the end of Hero Factory, he said. You know who that Hero was?"

Furno figured he knew how this story had to end. "It was Stringer, right?"

Bulk gave a harsh laugh. "Stringer? He's not that good at making speeches. No, that was me."

"You?" asked Furno, in disbelief. "I thought your philosophy was 'pound first, ask questions later'?"

"It is. But I like to know I'm pounding some-body for the right reasons."

A red light began flashing on the console. Three blips appeared on the tracking scope, clos-ing on the Hero craft from behind.

"Oh, look, company's coming," said Bulk.

"What do you think?"

"I think they're not here to escort us to a vaca-tion planet for a few weeks of fun in the sun," answered Bulk as he powered up the ship's weap-ons systems.

The three blips were drifting apart now, two of them moving to flank the Hero craft while the other stayed on its tail. Sensors indicated the ships had standard weaponry but powerful engines.

"The readout on the tech doesn't make sense," Furno reported. "Ships that old wouldn't have high-tech engines."

"Could have been a refit," Bulk pointed out. "They bought new engines or stole new engines. Anyway, means we won't be outrunning them, not without a lot of effort and a little luck."

The two flanking ships fired simultaneously, their laser blasts crossing each other in front of the Hero craft. "They've got guts," Furno said, "attacking a Hero Factory ship."

"You're forgetting, we don't look like a Hero craft," said Bulk. "We look like an old cargo ship that can't maneuver. Now watch this."

Bulk abruptly throttled back, slowing the ship down. The ships on the flanks shot forward. The one in the rear had to climb suddenly to avoid a collision. Bulk executed a sudden loop and came up behind the pursuing vessel. At the same time, he switched off the chameleon circuit. The image of a cargo ship wavered and disappeared, replaced by the reality of a fully armed Hero craft.

"I bet that got their attention," said Furno.

If Bulk expected the attacking ships to take off, though, he was mistaken. The ships maneuvered into a semicircle in front of the Hero craft, using reverse thrust to stay out of range of its weapons. Of course, that meant their blasts couldn't reach the Hero craft, either. They seemed satisfied to just keep their target penned in.

"They're stalling," said Bulk. "Why are they stalling?"

"Here's a better question," said Furno. "These are pirates, more than likely. Why are they willing to go head-to-head with Hero Factory? Usually, they run for the nearest nebula."

Bulk banked the ship right and tried to flank the pirate vessels. They responded by pulling back and taking a few almost-casual shots with their lasers. Bulk tried again, this time diving to get a clear line of fire at the undersides of the opposing ships. He did manage to do some damage to one vessel before they succeeded in pulling back.

"This is annoying," Bulk griped. "Keep this up and I'm going to get frustrated."

"We're wasting time," Furno said. "Let's just take them."

"You got it," said Bulk, hitting the thrusters.

The Hero craft vaulted forward. It had gone only a short distance when Bulk spotted a huge shape looming up ahead. He jerked the yoke of the ship, just avoiding a collision.

"What . . . is *that*?" he sputtered.

"A ship," said Furno. "A *really* big ship."

Bulk shook his head, as if doing that might make what was before his eyes vanish. It was a fully armed battle cruiser, the kind manufactured in the old days — before Hero Factory — when every planet had to defend itself. He didn't need sensors to know it had been fully reconditioned. In the hands of pirates, it was a major menace.

"Furno, get on the comm," said Bulk. "Scramble the message. We don't need our new friends out there listening in. Let Stormer know what we've just run into."

Bulk glanced down at the scanners and gave a low whistle. "They've got plasma cannons, lasers, mass drivers, and an electromagnetic pulse emitter — just like ours. One blast from that and everything mechanical shuts down for at least an hour."

Furno sent the signal. Stormer's response came back immediately. "Bulk, this is Stormer on scramble. Do not engage, repeat, do not engage. Stringer's situation takes priority. I'll send Rocka and Evo up."

Bulk didn't like the idea of running from a fight. Neither did Furno. But they both knew this was a fight they might not win, and if they lost, Stringer was as good as doomed.

"Hang on," said Bulk. "We're about to move, sudden and fast."

Bulk wrenched the controls, and the metal of the Hero craft screamed in protest as the vehicle executed a high-speed, 180-degree turnabout. The cruiser was more powerful, but nowhere near as maneuverable as the Hero Factory ship.

Before the startled pirates could react, Bulk and Furno were far gone.

It didn't take long for their foes to collect their wits and pursue. Laser fire flashed past the Hero craft, and mass-driver spheres launched by the cruiser impacted their rear shields. Bulk pushed the ship as hard as he could, trying to get every last ounce of speed out of the engines.

"We had to leave the cruiser behind," Furno reported. "But the smaller ships are gaining."

"Won't do them any good," said Bulk.

He steered the Hero craft around a small moon, putting the rocky orb between him and the pirates. In the few moments the pursuers were out of sight, Bulk activated the chameleon circuit again. This time, he made the Hero craft look like an asteroid floating in space.

Furno could see the outline of the ship change on the screen. "That's some trick," he said, smiling.

"Drains the heck out of the power reserves, but it's got its uses," Bulk replied.

When the pirate ships swept around the moon, they noticeably slowed, puzzled by the disappearance of their quarry. The three ships broke formation, trying to spot the Hero craft and failing. After several minutes, they turned and headed away, wondering how the Heroes had made their escape.

On board the Hero craft, Bulk allowed himself a small smile as he shut off the disguise device. "That's us, the disappearing Heroes. I'm plotting a course for Stringer's last-known location. Let's go before those losers come back."

As the Hero craft moved off, Furno leaned back in his chair. "I still wonder why, even with a cruiser, they would go after us. Everybody knows the hammer Hero Factory can bring down when it wants to."

"Do they?" Bulk answered. "I'm not so sure anymore. That breakout a while ago . . . a lot of robots lost faith in Hero Factory then. They expect us to keep the bad guys caged up, and if we can't do it . . ." His voice trailed off.

"But we recaptured all of the escapees," said Furno. "What's the problem?"

"They shouldn't have gotten out in the first

place!" Bulk snapped. "We screwed up. Now everyone is waiting to see if we'll screw up again. And until we prove we aren't going to, a lot of bad guys are going to push us to see if they can get away with it."

Furno thought about that. If the criminals of the galaxy stopped being afraid of Hero Factory, they would try bigger and bolder crimes. A lot of innocent robots could get hurt. "We need a win," he said finally.

"Right," agreed Bulk. "Got any worlds that need saving?"

"No," Furno answered. "But maybe Stringer does."

2

The Hero craft arrived in orbit around Tranquis VII. The planet consisted of one populated city, the capital, also called Tranquis. Furno tried radioing the control tower there for clearance to land, but got only static. The two Heroes glanced at each other.

"Nobody's home," said Furno.

"Scanners are reading a whole lot of nothing down there," said Bulk. "I guess their major export is rubble."

"Can you set her down near where Stringer's signal came from?"

"If there was a clear space bigger than a square foot around the spot, yeah . . . but there isn't. We may have to come down outside of the city and walk, or run, depending on what's waiting under all those rocks."

The Hero craft dropped out of space and pierced the veil of clouds that covered the city. Vision did not get any clearer after that, though, as the smoke from countless fires turned the atmosphere into a haze.

"They really need to fire their decorator," said Furno. "What a disaster area."

"Are you getting any traces of what caused this?"

Furno shook his head. "No radiation. No sign of weapons fire, other than some small arms — nothing like a bombardment from space. Atmosphere scan isn't showing any signs of plague or toxins. I'm not even showing signs of deactivated robots."

Bulk had a hard time believing that last part. "You mean everybody's still walking around, and this place looks like that? What a bunch of slobs."

Furno didn't smile at his comment. "I almost

wish we were seeing a standard disaster area. This is . . . creepy."

"Yeah, but, Furno, we're *Hero Factory*," Bulk replied. "Handling 'creepy' is in our job description. Better call in."

Furno switched on the ship's communicator. "Hero craft Four to Hero Factory, come in."

"This is Evo, Hero craft Four. Go ahead."

"We've reached Tranquis, Evo. The place is a mess," said Furno. "We're going in. Will contact you as soon as we have some idea of the situation on the ground."

"Got it," said Evo. "Good hunting, guys. Hero Factory out."

The Hero craft came in for a landing in a barren spot just past the city limits. Furno ran another scan of the immediate area, but still saw no signs of anything that would be fatal to robots. The two Heroes exited the ship, looking around warily as they did so.

"You think the ship will be safe here?" asked Furno.

"I've felt safer," Bulk admitted. "It's hard to know how to protect it when we don't know what we're protecting it from."

Together, the two Heroes moved out. Furno tried using his sensor pack to locate Stringer, and again got only static. He tried scanning on other frequencies, but that was no better.

"Something's jamming us," he told Bulk. "Every Hero Factory scanner frequency is just garbage. I'm getting a trace signal on a higher band, but it's too faint to read. . . . Our equipment isn't designed to pick that up."

"Then redesign it," said Bulk. "If it's just the bands we scan on that are jammed, then I'm guessing someone knew we were coming."

"They've got Stringer," Furno said. "And they knew we would come after him."

"That would be my guess," said Bulk. "So look sharp, kid."

The outskirts of the city presented just as bleak a picture from the ground as the interior had from the air. The place was at least half in ruins, with small fires burning every few blocks.

Here and there, a geyser of water rose from a broken water main. Even the buildings that were still standing had sustained damage. The rest were mostly just piles of rock.

"Looks like a cyclone went through here," said Bulk.

"Already thought of that," Furno answered. "On our way here, I checked the galactic weather. There were no disturbances in this region recently."

"Who says all this damage was recent?"

"Come on, Bulk," Furno said, with a trace of impatience. "Do you really think an entire vacation planet gets trashed and Hero Factory wouldn't know about it?"

Bulk looked around. "I'd say yeah."

"I'm betting this *just* happened in the last few days, or close to it," said Furno. "Whatever it was knocked out communications, which is why Stringer was sent here in the first place."

"All right, so where do we start looking?" asked Furno. "This place is huge."

"We start there," Bulk answered, pointing to

the huge communications tower. "Where else could he have been transmitting from?"

They started walking. It was a hot day on Tranquis, with a wind that caused the dust to swirl in mini-cyclones along the ground. The silence in the city was eerie. If not for the fact that they could hear their own metallic footfalls on the ground, the Heroes would have thought their audio receptors had broken down.

Furno had never seen anything like this. He had been on planets ravaged by floods, earth-quakes, even robot-made disasters, but each time the population had been hard at work cleaning up and rebuilding. Here, there was no sign of any-one. It was like everyone had just quit and left.

"Where are all the birds and animals?" Furno said. "Even if the robots are gone, you would think we'd see something alive."

"You don't know much about Tranquis VII, do you, kid? They had an environmental disaster here about ten years ago — wiped out most of the wildlife. Some folks said the planet would never be habitable again. But the robots here refused to leave. They stayed, worked hard, and built it into someplace others wanted to visit." Bulk looked around at the ruins. "We owe it to them to find out what happened here."

Furno quickened his pace just a bit. While continuing to look straight ahead, he said, "I think we're being followed."

Bulk knew better than to look around, but his hand hovered near his weapon. "Where?"

"Next block over," said Furno. "I saw a shadow slip from one building to the next."

"Armed?"

"Couldn't tell."

"Do we try and capture him?" asked Bulk.

"Let's make things interesting for him and see how far he's willing to go," Furno answered.

Using a combination of Furno's flame blast and Bulk's powerful drill, the two Heroes started to dig a tunnel beneath the street. When the initial hole was large enough, they vanished inside, continuing their work as they moved along. After fifteen minutes of digging and drilling, Furno said, "Has anyone followed us in?"

Bulk chanced a look over his shoulder. "No, I don't see anybody."

"Then he stayed up top, probably following the vibrations from your drill. Let me dig a while; I'm quieter," said Furno. "We'll go a little farther, then double back and see if we can catch him from behind up on the street."

The rock melted swiftly before Furno's flame. So far, they hadn't seen anything unexpected down here, just pipes and power cables and the other things society crams out of sight. Furno was just about to shut down his fire and signal Bulk to turn back when the wall before him crumbled completely.

Furno was so surprised at the sight of a chamber looming in front of him that he never noticed the dozen laser weapons pointed his way. Bulk saw them, though, and tackled Furno, yelling, "Down, kid!"

Devastatingly powerful beams of light lanced through the air above them, searing holes into the stone wall. Bulk and Furno were pinned down.

"You know, I was in a sewer once where they

had these really big ratbots," said Furno. "But they didn't arm them with lasers!"

"And those aren't rats," said Bulk. "They're security robots with advanced weaponry. I guess they don't like trespassers."

"Do they know who we are?"

"Better question is, do they *care* who we are?" said Bulk. "I have a feeling the answer is no."

Laser fire continued to pepper the area around the Heroes. One blast came close enough to make smoke rise from Bulk's shield.

"I say we rush them," said Furno.

"They'll punch a lot of little holes in your shield before you get more than three feet, then they'll do the same to you," Bulk said. "Hang on a second; I think I have an idea."

Bulk crawled across the tunnel floor and grabbed a piece of rock that had crumbled off the wall. He gave it a quick examination and then smiled.

"Thought so," he said to Furno. "This wall is made of likozite. Turn your flame on the wall and give it everything you've got."

Furno did as he was asked, focusing his fire-power on one spot on the stone wall. It required total concentration to heat the rock without making it explode, not easy to maintain while robots are firing lasers in your direction. But he did it, and when he was done, the likozite had become as smooth as glass.

"My turn," said Bulk. He suddenly sprang up, placing his head in line with the spot Furno had just fired upon. When one of the security robots fired, Bulk ducked. The laser bolt hit the mirrored surface and bounced back, hitting the sec-bot.

There was a moment's pause as the opposing force tried to figure out what had just happened. Bulk took advantage of the time to rip the glassy portion off the wall. He tossed it to Furno, saying, "Good old likozite—get it hot enough and you've got a nice piece of reflective glass that lasers bounce right off. *Now* we can charge."

Furno strapped his own shield onto his back and wielded the section of wall. Taking the lead, he ran forward, the laser blasts bouncing off the likozite. Bulk was behind him, staying low.

The security robots backed off, taking cover behind an assortment of crates in what had now opened up to be a wide corridor. Lights along the walls provided a dull illumination, enough to see this was no sewer or storm drain. Someone had constructed this with care.

Furno heard Bulk slip a rocket into the launcher on his drill weapon.

"Hey, what are you doing?" said Furno. "We don't want to blow these guys up."

"Relax, it's a flash-bang," Bulk replied. "Lots of light, lots of noise, no damage—just shakes them up a little."

Bulk launched the rocket, and he and Furno both shut down their optic and audio receptors for a few seconds. The rocket went off with a mind-numbingly loud sound and a searingly bright white flash that illuminated the entire corridor. Caught unprepared, the security robots staggered, unable to see to fire their weapons.

"Their vision will clear in a minute or so," said Bulk. "That gives us time to get out of here."

He was already on the move, heading back the way he and Furno had come. "What?" said Furno. "Don't you want to know what this was all about? Who are those guys? What is this place?"

"Sure I do," Bulk yelled back. "But we just tried going in through the front door, and how much fun was that? Next time, we try an upstairs window."

The two Heroes made it back out to the street. The sun was setting now. They took cover for a few minutes, keeping an eye on the tunnel to see if anyone pursued them. No one did. Nor was there any obvious sign of the being who had been following them. The city was just as quiet as it had been before they went underground.

Satisfied that they were alone for the moment, Bulk said, "We better camp for the night. I don't want to be wandering these streets in the dark until we know what's out there."

Furno wanted to argue—after all, it was urgent they find Stringer—but he knew Bulk was right. They wouldn't do their friend any good if they got injured or killed trying to make their way around a strange city at night.

"You want a fire?" he asked.

"No, I don't want to draw attention to ourselves. In fact, we're not going to stay at ground level at all." Bulk pointed to a nearby building, damaged but still intact. "We'll camp out on the roof. If someone wants to get at us, let them work for it."

Bulk and Furno entered the building through a door that had been broken open. The place was as quiet as a robot reclamation pile and as dark as a villain's heart. On the way to the roof, Bulk shined a flashlight into each room they passed, hoping to spot someone. But there was no one to be found.

There were no signs of a battle anywhere that the two could see. It did look like the occupants had left in a hurry, though. Equipment was scattered all over, chairs overturned, doors marked "Classified" left unlocked. Furno spotted a recharging station still active, as if someone had been in the middle of using it and just got up and left.

The one thing that really stood out was in

a corridor, in which some cleaning powder had spilled out of a bag in a maintenance closet. The powder had covered a portion of the floor and there were tracks in it of . . . something. It looked like it was a creature with multiple legs, perhaps some kind of a large spider.

"Well, something happened that they were all in a rush to see," commented Bulk.

"Or in a rush to run away from," Furno replied. "It's probably the same in the communications tower."

After twenty minutes of climbing, they reached the roof. The shroud of smoke that obscured the city masked the stars. The night air was cold, and both Heroes switched on internal heating units. Bulk volunteered to take first watch.

"Hey," Furno said after a little while. "Do you think Stringer is still alive?"

Bulk thought for a moment before he answered. "Furno, you wouldn't believe some of the stuff I've seen Stringer survive. Monsters, living planets, power-crazy villains, natural disasters—you name it, he's handled it. This place? The Stringer I know would laugh at it. Yeah, he's alive out there somewhere, don't worry. We'll find him."

Furno shut down his optic receptors and tried to rest. He couldn't stop wondering about how a thriving city on such a popular world could have been turned into a ghost town so quickly. What had struck this place, and did it have anything to do with those laser-happy security robots underground?

The sound of Bulk giving a low whistle brought Furno fully alert. "What is it?" he asked.

Bulk was at the edge of the roof, peering down at the street. "There's something moving down there," he said. "In fact . . . there's a lot of 'somethings' moving down there. I do believe we're surrounded."

ake sure the door is locked," said Bulk.

Furno did as he was told. There was a lock on the door, but it wasn't a very strong one. The Hero broke off a length of pipe and jammed it between the handle and the wall to make it harder for anyone to get through.

"What do you see?" he asked Bulk.

"Well, they've got two arms and two legs," Bulk replied. "Look like robots, but from up here, it's hard to tell what kind. They don't seem to be in any hurry, though."

"Huh?"

"They're just . . . wandering around, sort of

drifting into a ring around the building. I'm not seeing any weapons, nothing obvious anyway. But if we go back down, we're going to have to go through them. I'd be willing to bet you that's not a great idea."

Furno walked to the edge of the rooftop and glanced down. He could see some small figures moving for the door to the building. "They're coming in."

Bulk pointed down the side of the structure. "And they're climbing up."

Furno couldn't believe what he was seeing. The robots were actually punching handholds in the face of the building and pulling themselves up. About a half dozen had already passed the first few floors.

"Well, that's . . . disturbing," said Furno. "Next time, I pick the campsite."

"Any ideas?" said Bulk. "If Breez were here, she'd point out that we don't actually *know* they're hostile."

"Sure," said Furno, his voice dripping with sarcasm. "I always climb buildings in the middle of the night to give my friends a hug. We have two choices: stay and fight, or get out of here."

"It's a long jump to the next building," said Bulk. "Did you have an exit strategy in mind?"

"I thought I saw some good, strong electrical cable a few floors down, so, yes," Furno said, smiling.

The two Heroes unbolted the door to the stairs and raced down a couple of flights. Their visitors hadn't made it up this far yet. Furno found the roll of cable he was seeking and asked to borrow one of Bulk's rockets. Then he tied one end of the cable to the rocket. After he was done, he removed the mini-explosive from the head of the missile.

"Wow," said Bulk as he watched the operation unfold. "Does Stormer know you've gone insane?"

"Here," said Furno, handing the rocket back to his fellow Hero. "Launch this."

Bulk walked halfway down the hallway and kicked out a window. He could hear the tread of metal feet on the stairs. The robot mob was getting closer. Bulk took aim at the nearest building and launched the rocket. Without any explosive, it just buried itself in the stone wall of the building. The cable now stretched from the building the Heroes were in to the neighboring one.

Furno tied off the opposite end of the cable. Their improvised zip line was now ready for use.

"I'll go first," said Bulk.

"You will?"

"Sure. If I let you go first, and you wind up parts on the pavement, Stormer's going to want to know why I went along with this crazy idea in the first place," Bulk explained. "And since I don't have an answer for that, I'd rather take my chances with the line."

Bulk stepped out on the ledge, grabbed the line, and jumped into the night. He sailed across it, then let go as he neared the other building. He went feetfirst through a window. A couple seconds later, Furno could see him waving to signal he was okay.

Furno moved to follow him just as the door to the stairs swung open. He took one glance behind before making his escape. What he saw was enough to chill him to the Hero Core.

Bulk watched as Furno made it across to safety. As soon as the young Hero was back on his feet, he slashed the cable in two with his fire sword.

"Thought you might want to leave that up as a monument to your brilliance," Bulk joked.

But Furno wasn't laughing. "We need to call Hero Factory now. We either need a whole lot of backup, or we need to get off this world as soon as we can. We're sitting in the middle of a nightmare."

Dumacc was reviewing the footage for the third time. It didn't get any more entertaining with repeated viewings. Two intruders had managed to make it too far into the facility, and a supposedly crack team of security robots had been made to look like fools.

He froze the film on the scene of the two strange robots charging. Zooming in, he stared for a long time at the one wielding the massive drill. Things, he decided, were now officially worse than he had thought.

Turning to a security robot, he said, "Get Karter in here."

When Dumacc's top aide appeared, the first thing he saw was a blown-up image of the two intruders. Dumacc was pointing to the one bringing up the rear of the final charge. "I know him."

"Really?" Karter said. "Who is he? Does he work for a competitor?"

"You might say that," said Dumacc, failing to mask the anger in his voice. "He's Hero Factory. His name is Bulk. I can only assume the robot with him is a Hero as well."

"Why would Heroes be on Tranquis? And why would they attack our security team?" Karter asked. "Could they know why we're here?"

"Of course they know!" snapped Dumacc. "Why else would they visit this dump of a world?"

Karter frowned. "Shooting at them was very foolish. You know what kind of heat Hero Factory can bring down on our heads."

"What I know," Dumacc said sharply, "is that recent events have forced us to accelerate our timetable. Project Sunstorm is moving ahead, Karter, and it is your job to see that the work is undisturbed. That's why you were sent here. I was assured that you could keep potential obstacles like Hero Factory out of the way."

Now Karter's voice rose in response, tinged with anger. "There is no way anyone could have anticipated what's happened on this planet! With a disaster of this magnitude, maybe it was inevitable that Hero Factory or someone like them would arrive. But it's your security robots that are going to make them want to stay . . . and investigate. And you know what's going to happen if they find out about the project."

Dumacc turned away and walked into the main lab facility. A small team of robots was silently analyzing wave patterns on computer screens. Dumacc paused to join them, saying,

"It's too inconsistent. You need to bring down the spikes here and here and increase the power there."

"Dumacc, action will have to be taken," Karter persisted. "You can do it, or I will. Make your choice."

Dumacc looked at him with an expression that was both cold and, more disturbingly, devoid of any emotion at all. "As project leader, I decide what gets done. And my decision is that we do nothing for right now. We hope, for their sake, that they leave Tranquis . . . or, failing that, the forces on the surface keep them too busy to find this facility."

"If not," said Karter, "and if they learn things they aren't supposed to learn, then we will have to . . . deal with them."

"What are you saying?" asked Dumacc.

"You've been up top," said Karter. "You know what's going on up there. It would look like an accident. No one would even suspect anything different."

Dumacc changed the topic. "I need more

subjects for my tests. We need to know the 'whys' of what's happening on this planet."

Karter nodded. "I'll send security."

"Do it in the morning," Dumacc replied. "You know what it's like at night. We don't need to lose more security robots to what's out there in the dark."

Karter left to go inform the day watch commander. Along the way, he marveled at just how many things Dumacc had gotten wrong.

Yes, it would be best if the two Heroes just got in their Hero craft and left, but no sane robot would believe that would ever happen. Heroes don't run away from trouble. And if the menace up above, or anything else, were to injure them, Hero Factory would blanket the planet with agents to make sure justice was done. Project Sunstorm would surely be uncovered then.

That left the option of sending out security to try to take down two trained Heroes. As much as he respected the capabilities of the robots who guarded this facility, he knew they wouldn't win, not without a lot more luck than they were likely to get. No, there had to be another way . . . and maybe he knew what it was.

He approached the day watch commander. "Dr. Dumacc needs a half dozen more subjects. And we have another little problem I need to discuss with you. . . ."

"I know we have a problem—we have a lot of problems," said Bulk. "Which specific one are you so worried about, Furno?"

"Did you read Stormer's report on his last mission?" asked Furno. The two robots were on the move, having decided that getting to the communications tower couldn't wait until morning.

"Sure, I did. He, Rocka, and Breez ran into those nasty brains from outer space that can take you over if they land on your head. They'd hijacked the crew of the *Valiant*, a new battle cruiser, and were trying to crash the ship into Hero Factory. Our guys saved the crew and the brains wound up fried by the sun. What does that have to do with—?"

"The robots that followed us into that building," said Furno. "They had brains attached to their heads. Those creatures are back, and they're on this planet!"

Bulk's expression turned grim. "You're right. We need help, and lots of it."

The communications tower was in sight. The two Heroes raced inside and pounded up the stairs toward a transmission center. "As soon as we get a call out to Hero Factory, we find Stringer and get off-planet," said Bulk.

"He was right—this place needs to be quarantined," Furno answered. "We have to make sure the brains don't get off this world before Stormer and the team arrives."

They stopped at the first transmission room they came to, only to find the wiring had been torn out of the equipment. It was the same story in each of the next four rooms they visited. Someone had systematically wrecked the communication capabilities of the tower.

"This is pointless," said Furno. "We'd need at least a day to repair the damage here, and we don't have that sort of time. We'll have to leave the city and call in from the Hero craft."

"Don't bother."

Both Heroes turned at the sound. Standing in the doorway was Stringer.

"By now, the Hero craft has certainly been captured," he said. "It's got the new chameleon circuit, doesn't it? That will make things much easier."

The words were in Stringer's voice, but the thoughts behind them didn't belong to him. No, they came from the brain that was attached atop his head.

"Oh no . . ." said Furno.

"Listen, you piece of space garbage," growled Bulk. "Let our friend go and maybe I won't drop you off the roof and see how many times you bounce."

Stringer smiled. "Empty threats, metal thing. You can't harm me without harming your friend in the process. We both know you won't do that."

The controlled Hero leaned casually against the door frame. "Besides, even if you did stop me, we control this city," he continued. "You'll never get out of it alive."

"Pal, we've been the last ones standing in more fights than you can count," said Bulk. "Stormer says you brains get the knowledge of whoever you take over, and if that's true, then you know how many times Stringer and I beat the odds. You brains are no tougher than Von Nebula or the Witch Doctor or Speeda Demon or any of our other foes—you're just uglier."

"Bulk, enough," said Furno, turning to Stringer. "We've run into you . . . *things* before. What are you doing here? What is it you want?"

"Oh, we have what we want," said Stringer. "We have enough ships to get off this planet and go where we will. We have the body of a Hero to gain access to places no one else could enter. And now we have the opportunity to add two more Heroes to our forces. . . ."

Bulk took a step back and raised his weapon.

"I don't think so, gruesome. . . . Hats don't look good on me."

"You have no choice," said Stringer, taking a step forward. "Refuse and I can make this body jump out the window . . . or harm itself in any of a dozen ways."

Furno's flame sword roared to life. "Try it and you won't even leave any ashes, brain."

"I see you need persuasion," said Stringer. "Fortunately, some of my friends have come along with me."

A dozen robots came shambling down the hallway to assemble behind Stringer, each wearing a brain on its head. They were unarmed, but somehow the Heroes knew that didn't make them any less dangerous.

Furno glanced around. There was no way out of this room but the window, and a ten-story drop to the street. He and Bulk were going to have to fight, he realized.

And they were going to lose.

4

Stormer was beyond worried.

There had been no word from Furno and Bulk since their initial call-in. Rocka had managed to reroute some satellite imagery, bouncing it off a few different relays and sending an image of Tranquis back to Hero Factory. Furno hadn't been lying—the capital city looked like a disaster area. Now there were three Heroes missing in the middle of that mess.

"Are you getting any readout on the Hero craft?" he asked Evo. "Are they still on the planet?"

"Everything's jammed on the surface, but, yes, I think that it's still on the ground."

"I need more than you 'think' so," Stormer snapped. "We have Heroes missing in action. I want them found!"

"Yes, sir," said Evo. "Should I assemble a search team?"

Stormer pondered the question. His gut instinct was to send every available Hero out to find Bulk, Furno, and Stringer. But with no way of knowing what the trouble was, he might well be dispatching more Heroes to their doom.

"Not yet," he answered finally. "We sit tight for now. Monitor the satellites and all communications. Let me know the instant anything changes. We're just going to have to hope that whatever trouble our robots are in, they can find a way to get out of it."

Okay, how are we going to get out of this? Bulk thought to himself as he fought against the army of brain-controlled robots.

Bulk was more than just any Hero. He was

one of the best fighters in the history of Hero Factory, with a talent that was more instinctive than programmed. Bulk was skilled at doing an instantaneous analysis of an opponent, spotting his weak points, and anticipating his blows. It was a talent that had served him well for years. But he hardly needed it to tell that something was wrong here.

Stringer moved just like he always had, even with an alien brain in control. But these other robots moved like puppets controlled by an amateur puppeteer. Their motions were jerky and awkward, and their fighting style amounted to "smash and move on." Where Stringer darted, struck, and retreated, these others lumbered forward and kept going until they were pounded into the ground.

If I ever make it out of this room, Bulk thought, *I'm going to figure out why there's a difference between Stringer and the native robots, and I'll look like a genius. Right now, I guess I look like a punching bag to these guys, because that's sure what they're using me for.*

Furno was having his own problems, trying to fight off a horde of brain-controlled robots without setting the room, or the whole building, on fire. Stringer's controller had been right: They couldn't fight at full force knowing that the robots were innocent pawns of the brains.

Suddenly, laser fire erupted in the hallway. Caught by surprise, the mind-controlled robots piled out of the room, only to be met by devastating bolts of light. Led by Stringer, they retreated down an emergency staircase, pursued by what Furno could now see were more of the security robots he and Bulk had encountered earlier.

Great, he thought. *Out of the smelter and into the recycling forge . . . this day just keeps getting better.*

He and Bulk were bracing for a second fight when a robot walked into the room with his hands held out at his sides, a universal sign that he came in peace. There was no brain on his head and he wasn't a security robot. His blue-and-red coloring, thin frame, and lack of factory-issue weapons attachments (the blaster he carried was jury-rigged onto his hip) marked him as a B-1 model. B-1s were bureaucrats and administrators, usually employed by local governments.

Bulk, for one, wasn't buying it. *Maybe he looks like a B-1, even does the job, but I'd bet my last Hero Core that he isn't one. The way he moves, the way he's keeping an eye on us even as he offers friendship . . . he's fought before, and won. This one's dangerous.*

"My name is Karter," said the B-1 robot. "Sorry we were late. It took us a while to track you down."

"We weren't looking to leave a trail of oil," said Furno. "The last time we saw your robots, they were firing at us."

"An unfortunate mistake," said Karter. "As you saw, circumstances have turned Tranquis into a very perilous place. Naturally, our security forces are extremely alert these days. I've come to personally apologize for that incident and to invite you to visit our facility here. There are recharging stations there and it is completely safe from . . . uninvited guests."

"Yeah, we got that impression," said Bulk. "Do you have a subspace radio that works?"

"I'm sure something can be arranged," said Karter. "We can't afford to stay here much longer — more of those things will be converging on this building any minute. Are you willing to accompany me?"

"Sure, why not?" said Bulk. "What good is it being on a vacation planet if you don't go see the sights?"

Karter and his team of security robots led Bulk and Furno out into the street. Furno wasn't happy about the situation — he wanted to go after Stringer — but Bulk persuaded him that things wouldn't be that easy.

"I think there's more going on here than just the brains," said Bulk. "I have a feeling if we just take Stringer and run, we'll be missing the real rot on Tranquis."

As they traveled through the dark streets, both

Heroes spotted more robots with brains affixed to their heads. Like the others, they moved in a stiff, strange fashion, as if they were just learning to walk. The brains kept their distance from the security team, no doubt having learned the dangers of lasers in an earlier encounter.

Karter and the Heroes took a roundabout route to their destination, cutting through alleys and even slipping in and out of buildings. Once certain they were not being followed, Karter had one of the security robots pull up the grating over a storm sewer. He invited the Heroes to descend.

At first, it looked and felt like any other tunnel beneath a modern city—damp, dank, and a little cold. The major difference was that there were no rats or other vermin in sight, since they had all died with the rest of the wildlife a decade before.

After a few minutes' walk, though, things changed abruptly. One wall of the sewer slid aside to reveal an ultramodern laboratory, lined with computer banks and packed with robot technicians. Vats of fluid were bubbling away in one corner, while nearby robot scientists filed out of a heavy radiation chamber and submitted themselves for decontamination.

What really caught the attention of the two Heroes, though, was a large iron-glass cage in which three robots wandered around, each with a brain attached to his head.

Bulk gestured to the enclosure. "Trying to be the first on your block to collect them all?"

Karter gave a thin smile. "Those things are menaces. We're trying to find a way to cure the poor, unfortunate robots who have been victimized by the aliens."

Yeah right, thought Bulk. *Why don't I believe you?*

"As you can see, we have the technology down here to achieve miracles," Karter continued. "And that may be just what we need now."

Furno looked around. There was equipment here even the Hero Factory labs didn't have. He could imagine a lot of good could be achieved in a facility like this — probably a lot of bad, too. He kept his hand close to the hilt of his fire sword.

"But you didn't build all this in reaction to the brains," he said. "They haven't been on this planet for long, have they?"

"You're correct," said Karter, leading them deeper into the facility. "This was built several years ago in reaction to the disaster that struck here. But our research may prove useful in the current emergency. Let me show you something."

Karter waved his arm and an entire wall transformed into a video screen. Displayed on it was a vast array of charts and tables. "This was the situation on Tranquis right after the incident. As you can see, in the immediate aftermath, no organic life could survive here. Even robotic life was in danger from the toxicity in the air and water. Reclaiming this planet in such a short time was nothing less than incredible."

"If everything's fine now, what do they need you guys for?" asked Bulk.

"We're studying the causes of the disaster— pollution, reckless use of energy sources, failure to monitor internal chain reactions inside the planet—in order to keep it from happening again. We're also studying any long-term effects of the situation on the population. Believe it or not, that's where the brains come in."

"So, wait a minute, there were side effects to this environmental mess that are still lingering?"

"Yes," replied Karter. "Some are easy to spot, some aren't, but they are there in the native robots."

"And the brain connection . . . ?" asked Furno.

"Let me answer that one," said Bulk. "The robots on this planet are different now from standard ones, because of the disaster ten years ago. You didn't know how much of a difference that might make until the brains attacked, did you?"

"Go on," said Karter.

"Something is messing up the linkage between the brains and the robots here. That's why they shamble around like they're half-dormant. The brains can shut the robots' minds down, but can't get full control of the bodies. They can't make the robots do what they want them to do."

"Exactly," said Karter, walking up to the clear wall of the cage. One of the mind-controlled robots saw him and began pounding on the opposite side of the wall, but the iron-glass was too tough to crack. "The robots of Tranquis have a partial immunity to the power of the brains. We're hoping to find a way to develop a full immunity to protect the galaxy from these monsters."

"How can we help?" asked Furno.

Karter looked a little uncomfortable, or at least he was trying to, as he said, "By staying out of the way."

"You want to try that again?" said Bulk, with more than a little anger and frustration in his voice.

"Listen, we are doing important work here," explained Karter. "Your presence is stirring up the brain creatures. They're getting more aggressive and harder to handle. That puts our personnel in danger and jeopardizes what we are trying to achieve here. It would be better for all concerned if you left Tranquis."

Bulk looked at Furno. Knowing how the fiery Hero was likely to react, Bulk stepped forward before Furno could do anything. "Maybe you don't understand. One of ours is on this world and the brains have him. Now, I don't give a broken bolt about your work, but I do care about my friend. And we're not leaving this planet without him."

The news that there was another Hero on Tranquis appeared to take Karter by surprise. Still, his response was swift. "I'm sorry to hear about your fellow Hero, but that doesn't change the facts. As a representative of the local government here, I could make you leave. No one requested help from Hero Factory, and it's not needed."

"How dare you—" Bulk began.

Now it was Furno trying to keep his friend from doing something rash. "Look around, Karter—your city is in ruins and you've got alien-controlled robots on a rampage. You're not going to stop that with test tubes and computer screens. You not only need us, you need a whole lot more of us!"

"This is ridiculous," said Bulk. "I'm invoking

my authority as the ranking member of Hero Factory here. I'm ordering an evacuation off-planet of anyone not infected by a brain, in an effort to stop this menace from spreading. We'll be calling in reinforcements, and you and your team will be escorted to a safe haven until the crisis is over."

Before Karter could answer, there came the sound of a dozen laser rifles powering up. Furno and Bulk turned to see a science robot flanked by security guards, all of them aiming weapons at the Heroes.

"I'm afraid that's not how this is going to end," said the head science robot.

"Dumacc, is this necessary?" said Karter to the science robot. "I'm sure Bulk and Furno are willing to be reasonable."

"Actually, we're not," said Bulk. "And I'd suggest aiming those things in another direction if you don't want to wind up eating them."

"Please, Hero," said Dumacc. "You'll be molten metal before you get anywhere near us, and you know it. We have no interest in hurting you, just confining you until we are finished with our work."

"This facility isn't designed to be a prison," said Karter. "Let me talk to them. I am sure we can come to some peaceful solution."

The words spoke of compromise, but the look on Karter's face was of well-controlled fury. *I guess he and this Dumacc character don't get along,* Bulk said to himself. *Maybe we can use that later.*

"They can stay under guard in empty quarters," said Dumacc, "or we can put them in the cage with the brains — their choice."

"We should have fought," said Furno.

He and Bulk were sitting in an unfurnished room off a side corridor in the complex; their weapons and shields had been taken away. Two security robots were out in the hallway, making sure they couldn't leave.

"Maybe," Bulk answered. "But they have a lot more than twelve guards. Do you really think we could have taken all of them, before a lucky blast got us? Learn to pick your fights, kid. We're alive, and when the time is right, we'll break out of here, don't worry."

"I don't get it," said Furno. "What's this all about?"

"Karter wanted us to leave with a smile on our faces, content that everything was under control here. He didn't want more Heroes on Tranquis," said Bulk. "But now that we've seen the inside of this place, I don't think Dumacc wants us leaving at all."

"Why not? What are they doing that's so secret?"

"Kid, kid," said Bulk, shaking his head. "Nobody's told the truth to us on this planet for more than five minutes at a time. They said their little group was formed as a response to the environmental catastrophe that hit this planet. Well, stop and think—what if that's not true? What if the truth is that they *caused* the disaster, and whatever they're doing now is likely to cause another one?"

"Wow," said Furno, the full impact of what Bulk was saying hitting him like a cannon shot. "But you don't have any proof of this. . . ."

"I had twelve laser rifles pointed at my face," Bulk growled. "That's proof enough for me. So listen up — we're going to save Stringer, beat the brains, and then before we go, we're going to bust Dumacc and Karter's little research project wide open. You with me?"

"All the way," said Furno. "So, what time is the jailbreak?"

5

The thing that controlled Stringer was thinking very dark thoughts.

All around, robots wearing brains wandered aimlessly around the badly damaged hotel Stringer had made his headquarters. They would respond to orders, he had discovered, but only with difficulty and only if the orders were something as simple as, "Go smash that." The rest of the time, they ambled around destroying whatever they ran across.

What that meant was that much of what he had told Furno and Bulk in the communications tower had been bluff. Yes, the brains had access to both the Hero craft and other ships. Yes, the brains could, in theory, get off the planet. But Stringer was the only one with enough control of his host robot to be able to pilot a ship. Taking a big ship would be impractical, since the other robots couldn't crew it, and a small ship would mean leaving most of the controlled robots behind. Neither option was very appealing.

The brains had discovered shortly after their arrival that something was wrong here. The robots here were different from those found elsewhere: They couldn't be properly controlled. It was pure luck that damage to the communications grid had resulted in a Hero being sent here and subsequently captured.

"Braining" Bulk and Furno would have been useful, providing two more skilled pilots. Since they had been rescued by that mysterious team of security robots, Stringer needed a new plan. To be efficient, he had come up with two.

Hero Factory was about to get another emergency call from the missing "Stringer," pleading for more assistance. A wave of Heroes would show up, and immediately get captured by the brains.

In the meantime, the reason for the security robots' existence was going to be uncovered and their base tracked down. Whatever they were doing here, the brains would find out about it and use it as part of their plan of conquest.

Stringer got up. It was time to issue orders. He hoped it wouldn't take two hours to make the others understand, like last time. He did, after all, have an important call to make.

S-12 flattened against the side of a building and carefully looked around the corner. Satisfied there were no "mind-controlled" robots around, he beckoned for his squad to follow him as he moved out into the street.

As a top-of-the-line security robot, S-12 was programmed to deal with any threat, from a natural disaster to a robot revolt. While the notion of an alien-controlled population was something new, the basic truths of the job remained the same: detain, defend, demolish. The underground laboratory was to be protected at all costs, and sometimes "protecting" meant going after the enemy before they were at the gates.

Today, S-12's squad was carrying out a mission they had done a few times before: securing prisoners for transport back to the lab. It could be dangerous work, since the mind-controlled could be wild and unwieldy. Fortunately, they had never shown any talent for strategy or tactics. It was fairly easy to trick them into ambushes, after which they could be subdued with electro-nets.

Often enough, the biggest challenge was just finding some to capture. They rarely ventured out during the day, but their numbers were too great at night to risk a confrontation. The security robots had to rely on catching stragglers during daylight hours, though these were becoming harder and harder to come by.

S-12 wasn't entirely sure that more mind-controlled robots were really going to help the scientists. They had already discovered that there was no way to get the brains off without doing damage to the host body. Nothing seemed to be able to persuade the brains to abandon the bodies, either. He had heard Dumacc and others speculating that, in the same way the bodies were fouled up by the takeover, perhaps the brains' thought processes were fouled up, too. The aliens no longer knew what was good for them, so they stayed with bodies that weren't proving very helpful. And so far, the quest to find out what made the Tranquis robots partially immune to control hadn't produced much in the way of results.

Still, it wasn't his job to question — just to act.

His theorizing was cut off by the sight of two robots sporting brains about a block away. Since his squad had the pair outnumbered three-to-one, S-12 decided there was no need for an elaborate trap. They would just charge and take the robots captive.

The security team broke into a run, lasers and nets at the ready. The two mind-controlled robots spotted them and started shambling away, moving as fast as they were able. In typical slow-witted fashion, they headed into a walled-in courtyard, effectively trapping themselves.

"Deploy nets," said S-12 as he led his squad through the courtyard entrance.

The two pursued robots were just standing there, as if they didn't have a care in the world. A moment later, the security team realized why: Other mind-controlled robots were lining the walls. A half dozen of them were carrying brains in their hands, ready to affix them to the security squad's heads.

As the alien-controlled robots closed in from every side, S-12 realized that the next time he saw home base, he would be under the control of an alien brain. All his skills and weaponry would be used to attack the very thing he was duty-bound to protect. In his last moment of free consciousness, his finger stabbed a button on his belt, sending an alarm signal back to the lab.

At least now they'll know, he thought. *When we come knocking at the door . . . don't let us in.*

Word of Stringer on the comm system brought Stormer to the command center on the run.

"Just came through, sir," said Evo. "He's broadcasting from the Hero craft, but we still can't get a fix on its location."

"Put him on," Stormer replied.

There was a loud hiss, a harsh crackle of static, and then Stringer was saying, "— Factory! Stringer calling Hero Factory! Do you read me?"

"This is Stormer. Go ahead, Stringer, what's your situation?"

"Desperate," Stringer answered. "Bulk and Furno have been captured by a rebel group. They have already wrecked much of the city and are planning to ransom both Heroes back to Hero Factory, in exchange for ships and weapons. I managed to escape to send out this warning, but I don't know how much time I have before they find me!"

"Can you get off-planet?" asked Stormer.

"No way. I'm not leaving Bulk and Furno. You need to send more Heroes, Stormer, as many as you can!"

"I can send Rocka and Breez in as an extraction team," said Stormer. "They can get the three of you out of there. Give me your coordinates."

"Negative," Stringer replied. "We need more than two Heroes and one more Hero craft. These rebels are out of control — they need to be crushed. We're the only ones who can do it!"

Evo glanced at Stormer, with a "what is he talking about?" expression on his face. Stormer's face was a mask, impossible to read.

"All right," the Alpha Team leader said. "Stay on this channel for as long as you can, Stringer. I'll see what resources we have available. Stormer out."

Evo cut off the broadcast. As Stormer turned to leave, Evo said, "Should I forward you the duty roster, sir, so you can start assembling a team?"

"No," Stormer said flatly.

"Begging your pardon, team leader, but what about Stringer . . . ?"

Stormer stopped at the door and looked back at Evo. "That wasn't Stringer, Hero. He'll look like him and sound like him, but if you run into him, you better use your blaster first. Understand?"

"Yes, sir."

Stormer left the room. Evo was left to wonder just what his team leader had meant, and if they would ever be seeing Stringer again.

Stormer sat alone in the dark. On his desk was every satellite image of Tranquis that Rocka had been able to find, as well as records of ship and communications traffic in the area for the last thirty-six hours.

All of it combined to produce a maddening amount of nothing. There was precious little information on which to base a decision. He would have to rely on instinct. Normally, in these situations, he could rely on the counsel of Bulk and Stringer, the two veterans on his team. With them both gone, he was wrestling with the situation alone.

His door buzzer sounded. A moment later, Zib, Alpha Team's Mission Manager, came in.

"Sorry to interrupt," said Zib. "I need a status update on the team. If Alpha is short-handed, I can shift missions to other teams."

"We're down three," Stormer replied.

"Estimate on when they'll be back?"

"Unknown."

Stormer regarded Zib for a minute. In all the years he had known the Mission Manager, Zib had never offered advice without being asked, or presumed to tell a team leader how to do his job. Yet he had seen it all, dating back to the early days of Hero Factory. Stormer suddenly realized that Zib might be the perfect robot to talk to.

He laid out the entire story as he knew it, which wasn't much. When he was done, Zib said, "How do you know it wasn't Stringer?"

"Stringer would never call for rebels to be crushed—he's more likely to be on their side," Stormer replied. "He was either being forced to say all that, or . . . he's not himself. We both know how that could happen."

"And Bulk? Furno?"

"They're probably prisoners," Stormer conceded. "But not of any rebellion. I think that's all a fiction, designed to lure more Heroes there. So . . . if I send in another team, I may be dooming them. If I don't, then Stringer, Bulk, and Furno may be lost. I'm having a hard time finding a way to win."

Zib was silent for a full minute. Then he said softly, "Maybe you're too close to this situation. Maybe you need to be more . . . long-range in your thinking. Control what you're able to control. Think about it, and if you need to talk again, I will be in the command center."

Zib departed. Stormer stared at the images of Tranquis and reflected on what Zib had said. Long-range thinking . . . control what you can control . . . long-range . . . control . . .

"Of course!" said Stormer, springing to his feet and heading for the door. "The prototype Hero craft!"

The alarm was sounding all over the underground complex on Tranquis. Security teams moved into position at all entrances, science robots were hustled into safe rooms along with as much of their research as they could transport, and every wing of the complex went on lockdown.

An agitated Dumacc found Karter in the main lab, overseeing a data transfer of the day's information into a secure computer located in another location. He moved quickly, but there was no trace of panic in him.

"Is all this really necessary?" demanded Dumacc. "It's disrupting our work!"

"We received a Level One alert from a security robot in the field," Karter said without looking at Dumacc. "We can only assume he and his team have been captured. You certainly know what that means."

Dumacc did indeed. His theory was that, under normal circumstances, the brains gained whatever knowledge their host possessed. A problem with the linkage had prevented that from happening with Tranquis inhabitants, but the security robots were recent arrivals. If the brains absorbed their knowledge, they would know the entire layout of the complex, including the secrets of every security system.

"Forget the data transfer," said Dumacc. "We have to do a purge. Erase all of it."

"You know I don't have the authority to do that."

"I'm giving you a direct order. Do it!" snapped Dumacc.

Karter turned and looked at the scientist with the same expression one might use on a particularly annoying insect. "I've been content to play right-hand robot to you all this time, for the sake of appearances. But you and I both know I don't take orders from you. The *group* I do answer to wants this information intact."

"If the brains attack and get ahold of it—"

"I don't think there's any 'if' about it," Karter said, going back to his work. "If the brains know what our S-12 units know, then they will attack. This data will be safely transferred by then, and after that, what happens to us . . . to this facility . . . won't matter anymore. My true bosses will simply build a new place elsewhere and the work will resume."

Dumacc staggered a step. He couldn't believe what he was hearing. "So you're going to, what, just surrender this facility, all this equipment, to the brains?!"

Karter flashed a thin smile. "Of course not. We will fight to the finish, if only so that the brains will believe there is still something of value here to fight for. During the course of the battle, any equipment that might be of use to the brains will 'accidentally' be destroyed. We have no chance of winning the fight, but we will accomplish what we have to—the research will survive and the brains won't be looking for a second lab."

A horrible thought sprang to life in Dumacc's mind. He didn't want to say it, but he couldn't help himself. "Wait . . . if we both know about the data transfer, and the brains get us, then they'll know, won't they?"

Karter's smile turned ice-cold. "There's that 'if' again. Yes, that's what would take place . . .

if we both lived long enough to be captured. But it's a funny thing about battles . . . accidents happen all the time . . . sometimes really bad ones."

Dumacc turned away and hurried from the lab, his mind racing. What could he do? Escaping to the outside was impossible now, with all entrances and exits sealed and the mind-controlled robots probably on the march through the streets above already. He was effectively trapped.

And doomed, he thought. *There's no doubt what Karter means. He'll destroy us both to keep us away from the brains.*

Try as he might, Dumacc couldn't think of a way out. Karter was right, the brains would attack and they would win and—

Unless they don't, he suddenly thought. *If they could just be beaten . . . but how?*

Then he remembered that he already had the means of defeating the brains at his fingertips. He just had to get Bulk and Furno to do it.

Bulk lay on the floor of the Heroes' improvised prison cell. He wasn't moving. Furno crouched over him, shouting, "Come on, Bulk, hang on! Hero Factory needs you!"

The veteran Hero didn't respond.

Furno rushed to the locked door and started to pound on it. "Hey, you out there! We need help! My friend is dying!"

The voice of a security robot came through the door. "What's the problem?"

"His Hero Core is running down. We were told there were recharging stations in this complex. He needs to get to one fast, or he's not going to make it!"

There was a pause. Then the guard said, "Back away from the door."

Furno took a few steps back. The door slid open and two security robots came in. One kept a laser on Furno while the other knelt down to examine Bulk. As he moved in close to peer into Bulk's optic sensors, the Hero's arm suddenly shot up and grabbed the security robot by the throat.

"Surprise!"

The other guard moved to aim his laser at Bulk, but Furno sprang forward and disarmed him with a quick chop to the wrist. Bulk tossed his captive aside and grabbed the laser.

"Okay, everyone take it easy," he said. "We want our weapons and shields, and you want to stay in one piece, so I think we can make a deal here."

Before the captured guards could answer, a third guard appeared in the doorway, laser rifle leveled at the Heroes. As his finger tightened on the trigger, there was a flash of light from behind him. He fell forward into the room, unconscious. Standing behind him, laser blaster in hand, was Dumacc.

"Oh, I was hoping to run into you," said Bulk.

Dumacc ignored him, instead addressing the other two guards. "Stand down. I'll take responsibility for these prisoners. Go manage the Number Four western entrance." When they hesitated, he added, "Do it!"

This time, the two security robots complied. When they were gone, Furno said, "So now what? We get blasted 'trying to escape,' or do you not even need an excuse on this planet?"

Dumacc lowered the blaster. "I need your help. This whole complex is in danger from the brains, and you're the only ones with any chance of surviving a fight with them."

"As I recall, you were ready to throw us to the brains yesterday," said Bulk. "Why should we believe anything you say? Let me tell you something, *saving* this place is not on my list of things to do. Wrecking it, on the other hand . . ."

Dumacc glanced down the corridor. For the first time, Furno noticed he looked nervous. "We don't have much time. Those two guards will report in to Karter, and more will be on their way to keep you two locked up. If you're going to escape, it has to be now."

"Fine," said Bulk. "But you'll go first. I don't want you behind me."

The three exited, with Dumacc up front and Bulk bringing up the rear. "I'll take you to your weapons."

"If you're so worried those security robots are going to tell on you, why didn't you blast them, too?" asked Furno.

"We're going to need as many lasers as we can get if we're going to make it through this fight," Dumacc answered.

They reached a vault set into a recess in the corridor. Dumacc started to punch in an access code. "Don't bother," said Bulk, punching a hole in the door and yanking it off its hinges.

Inside were Bulk's shield and drill, as well as Furno's shield and fire sword. They armed themselves, then Bulk turned to Dumacc. "This is as far as we go with you."

"What?" cried Dumacc. "Didn't you hear what I said? Everyone in this facility is in grave danger!"

"Ever think maybe everyone in this facility deserves to be? We're here to rescue our friend and then close the lid on this planet until the rest of Hero Factory gets here," said Furno. "Hauling your metal frame out of the furnace isn't part of our mission."

Desperation consumed Dumacc's features. Furno expected him to yell or threaten, but all the scientist did was slump against the wall in defeat. "Then it's over. I may as well let Karter do what he plans to do. . . ."

"Listen to me," Bulk said in a softer tone. "You want help? We need answers. What's the story with this place, and why would the brains want it? I thought all they wanted was off this rock."

Dumacc nodded. "Probably they did, until yesterday. But by now, they know the truth, and they're coming for us."

"Tell us," said Furno. "We need to know whatever they know."

"All right, all right," said Dumacc, sagging to the floor. "It hardly matters now."

Dumacc, Bulk, and Furno were in a small lab. The scientist sat at a computer terminal, punching up images as he talked.

"It was a good idea at the start," he explained. "It's hardly news to you that some planetary governments are worried about depending too much on Hero Factory, and want some kind of protection that they can control."

"Yeah," said Bulk. "Their faith in us is overwhelming."

"Think about it," Dumacc said sharply. "You can't be everywhere at once. And what about all the Heroes who have gone bad? What if the whole organization became corrupt? Who would be able to stop you?"

Bulk hated to admit it, but Dumacc did have

a point. It just wasn't one that anybody from Hero Factory liked to think about.

"I thought the plan was to build a fleet of ships to defend against any menaces," said Furno. "That ship, the *Valiant*, that got launched recently was supposed to be one of them, wasn't it?"

Dumacc laughed, a harsh, almost contemptuous sound. "That was all just for show. The planetary governments—my real bosses—built one ship, and that's all there was ever supposed to be. It was all just a cover for Project Sunstorm."

"Sunstorm?" said Bulk. "Cute name. Does it mean what it sounds like?"

Dumacc brought up an image of a sun, with tendrils of white-hot gas exploding from its surface. "The sun in this system is known for its solar flares. Project Sunstorm was created to tap into the power of those flares and turn them into a weapon."

He hit a button and the scene changed to an illustrated schematic of a mirrored satellite system. "This was going to be the final product. Solar flares would be triggered using mini-rockets fired from a main satellite. The flares would then be bounced off satellites equipped with orbital mirrors to strike wherever and whatever we wished. The satellites are the best that could be built, even shielded against electromagnetic pulses and other forms of interference."

"So what went wrong?" asked Bulk.

"What do you mean?"

"Come on," Bulk replied. "Something always goes wrong."

Dumacc shifted uncomfortably in his seat. "Our first attempt to control a flare . . . well, it didn't live up to expectations. It approached too close to Tranquis, and we think the resulting radiation had some serious environmental effects. But subsequent tests have been much more successful. On top of that, it's possible that radiation helped make the natives partially immune to the brains' control."

"I'm sure they'll be thrilled to hear that," said Furno. "So let me get this straight—you figure the brains know all about Sunstorm now and are going to seize control of it?"

Dumacc nodded. "If they get hold of that system, no one will be able to stop them. They can turn this part of the galaxy into an impregnable base from which to launch invasions on countless worlds."

"Then I guess we better not let them have it," said Bulk. "Let's get to work."

Stringer stood at a window of the communications tower, looking out over his city. Tranquis belonged to the brains now, or soon would — the underground laboratory complex was the last haven of any resistance. Once it was seized, and the secrets of Project Sunstorm were his, Hero Factory would fall and so would the rest of the civilized galaxy.

Only one thing worried him: Stormer had not radioed back to say he was sending more Heroes. Stringer was counting on him to do that, both as a way to whittle down Hero Factory's numbers and to gain more skilled pilots for the brains' cause. Had Stormer somehow gotten suspicious?

It didn't matter, he decided. Only a Hero craft would have enough firepower to do any damage to his robot army, and the only Hero craft on the planet was in the hands of mind-controlled robots. By the time Stormer sent more ships to rescue his Heroes, Sunstorm would be active. Any approaching vessel would have to surrender or be destroyed.

Even now, his robots were on the march, led by the security robots they had recently captured. There was nothing left now but the fighting. If the brains showed some mercy, the battle would be over swiftly and the residents of the complex would all survive to be mind-controlled themselves.

It was almost too bad that the brains had no mercy to show. . . .

Bulk and Furno stormed into the main laboratory. A startled Karter looked up from the data transfer terminal, his hand immediately going for the blaster on his hip. Bulk grabbed his wrist before he could get the weapon, saying, "Nah, you don't want to do that. You want to do this."

With that, he brought Karter's hand down on the terminal, smashing a hole in the delicate machine.

"You were right, he did want to do that," said Furno, relieving Karter of his blaster. "And he did it so well, too."

"What's the meaning of this?" Karter fumed. "I'll register a complaint about your conduct with Hero Factory!"

"Then you'll be doing it from a cell," said Bulk. "Irradiating an entire planet? Building illegal weapons systems? Doing research on a hostile alien species without authorization? Oh, you've been a bad robot, Karter, you and your pal."

Furno went out into the corridor and brought in Dumacc, who had been tied up with cable. "He switches sides so often that we got tired just watching him."

Bulk shoved Karter into a chair. "Now let's

talk about how we're going to keep this complex from being overrun by robots with brains. How long until they get here?"

"Ten minutes, maybe less," Karter answered. "But we haven't got the robot-power to beat them. What you're doing is pointless."

Bulk smiled. "Nah, it's not. See, you were fighting to lose, because you wanted the brains to think whatever they found here was all there was. Hero Factory only fights to win . . . and that's exactly what we're going to do."

Nearby, Furno had patched into the main computer network and was studying the security systems. "Doors are a foot thick and they're on an automatic lock," he reported.

"Pop quiz, kid," said Bulk as he did a quick scan of the lab's equipment. "Why is an automatic lock good for us?"

Furno thought for a few seconds. Then he smiled and said, "The doors have wiring in them. Overload it and we can electrify the doors."

"Get started," Bulk ordered. "Sunstorm is obviously out—we're not looking to incinerate the entire city. But there has to be something here we can use. . . ."

Karter laughed. "I tried to do you a favor. I tried to get you two off this planet. Now you can get overrun like the rest of us, while you pretend there's something you can do to stop it."

"I think I've got an idea," said Furno as he finished cranking up the voltage in the doors. "I think there is something here we can use against the brains."

"Spill it, kid," said Bulk.

Furno pointed at Karter. "Him."

"What?" snapped Karter. "If you think—"

"Quiet down, you," Bulk said. "What have you got in mind, Furno? And make it quick, we're short on time."

"It's simple," said Furno. "The brains want Project Sunstorm, but all they have is security bot knowledge of it—not the smarts they need to make the weapon work. For that, they need Dumacc, or one of the technicians . . . or Karter."

"Gotcha," said Bulk. "Why beat their brains out—pardon the pun—trying to get in here if they can grab him out there?"

Furno hauled Karter to his feet. "You're going for a little run. But don't go too fast — Bulk's an old model and might have a hard time keeping up with you."

"Hey!" snapped Bulk, in mock anger.

"At least some of the brains will go after you," Furno continued to his prisoner. "That will buy the security forces in here some time."

"And what are you going to do? Run and hide?" sneered Karter.

"No, I'm going after Stringer. Because I just might know how to save Tranquis, and I need him to help me do it."

A small group of mind-controlled robots marched in a circle around the Hero craft. It was incredibly dull work, but the robots didn't notice. With the weak linkage and the subsequent damage to their thought processes, the brains just did what the controlled Stringer told them to do. Bulk and Furno couldn't be allowed to leave the planet with what they knew, not unless they had the alien brains on their heads.

The ship had been very quiet all this time and no one had tried to board it. The robots would shuffle around and around it for months without a break, if they had to, unless something happened to make them stop. But what were the odds of that?

Pretty good, as it turned out . . .

One moment, the Hero craft was a space vessel. The next, it was a winged, six-headed solar-steel dragon, the kind that stalked the space lanes and fed on any organic life it ran across. The average robot wouldn't give one a second thought, since they wouldn't be on the menu, but the brains weren't robots. In this case, they were potential snacks.

Dull-witted as they might be, the brains knew this monster wasn't something to mess with. Their host bodies couldn't run, but they made them shamble away from the creature as fast as possible. The beast was firing lasers from its eyes, narrowly missing the few stragglers and spurring them to catch up to the rest.

Once the mind-controlled robots were gone, the monster vanished, to be replaced once more by the Hero craft. Back at Hero Factory, Stormer was pleased — the chameleon circuit on board the ship had just faced its toughest test, and passed. He couldn't be sure the brains would fall for the illusion of the monster, but based on the remote sensors, they had fled. That meant they wouldn't be warning anyone about what was about to happen.

The Hero craft powered up and rose from the ground, running lights blinking on. It slowly ascended to a hundred feet in the air, then started to move toward the city. Controlled by Stormer from base, it was about to give the brains a few surprises.

Seated at the main console in the control center of Hero Factory, Stormer kept an eye on the instruments. With the array of sensors and other equipment, he could pilot the Hero craft remotely almost as well as if he were seated in the cockpit.

They have three of ours, he thought as he charged the ship's weapons. *Here's where we start getting them back.*

Karter had been many things in his life: a spy, a thief, a deal-maker, even, for a brief time years ago, an actual assistant to a scientist.

This was the first time he had ever been a target.

Bulk and Furno had been able to access the plans for the underground base, which Karter knew by heart. Then they found a second set of plans buried under the programming of the first, which revealed there was a secret passage on the eastern edge of the complex that led to the surface. Karter had had no idea that was there. Apparently, the robots behind the building of the place were even better at keeping secrets than he was.

Of course, the security robots didn't know about the passage, either, which meant the brains didn't know about it. The two Heroes hustled him out of the complex. All around they could hear the distinctive sound of mind-controlled robots walking slowly and steadily toward their destination.

"You realize if I survive this, you are going to regret doing it," Karter hissed.

"Not a smart thing to say to the robot whose job it is to make sure you survive it," Bulk answered. "Get moving. These things may be slow, but they're stubborn, and you'll get tired before they will. Remember: Try to lead them into spots where I can ambush them."

"What if they ambush you?"

"Then you'll wind up with a brain on top of your head," Bulk shot back. "And having any sort of brain will be a first for you."

Furno wished his friend luck. He knew Bulk's job was impossible — you couldn't stop this many mind-controlled robots by fighting them a few at a time. You had to take them all out at once.

Karter ran out into the street. Almost immediately, he was spotted by four controlled robots. One of them was a security robot from the complex, and he was much faster and more agile than the others. Karter wouldn't be able to outrun him, so that left relying on Bulk.

He cut through an alley and then another, following the route the Heroes had suggested. Bulk was supposed to be positioned up ahead, waiting for the right moment.

Karter turned left into a dead-end street. The four robots were closing in on him and there was no sign of the Hero. He was calculating the odds of taking them all on himself, and they weren't encouraging. Of course, Dumacc wouldn't have even made it this far.

There was a loud rumble and a violent tremor beneath his feet. The abandoned building at the mouth of the street suddenly collapsed into a huge pile of rubble, trapping the robots on the narrow avenue with their prey. Before they could come too close to Karter, the pavement beneath their feet collapsed and they fell into a deep pit.

A few moments later, Bulk drilled up from beneath the street, grinning. "Okay, four down, a few thousand to go!" he said.

Karter took a deep breath and got ready to start again.

Furno was not looking forward to this part of the job.

Stringer was a veteran Hero, one of the first members of Hero Factory. Despite his modesty, he was known to have accomplished hundreds of vital missions and it could easily be said that the galaxy owed him a great debt. He was a cunning strategist, an agile fighter, and a master of sonics.

And now he was controlled by a brain from outer space.

That brain had access to every bit of knowledge he had about Hero Factory and its operations. It also had his robotic "muscle memory," enabling it to use his body to execute fighting moves. Furno would be up against the equivalent of an evil Stringer . . . and although the younger Hero had more than proven himself, in his core he wasn't sure he could win this fight.

But I have to try, he told himself. *If I don't, Stringer is lost and so is this planet. This is what he would want me to do.*

He stuck to the shadows on his way to the communications tower. It was the last place they had seen Stringer and the logical place for him to be if he was directing the attack against the complex — it afforded a view of the whole city. Plus, it "fit" somehow that a Hero whose powers derived from sound would be using a broad-casting center as his headquarters.

Too late Furno realized what else that choice of a headquarters might mean. A powerful wave of sound erupted from speakers mounted on the tower and knocked him flat on his back. He'd had his audio receptors turned up to make it easier to pick up hostile robots sneaking up on him, which made the attack doubly painful.

Struggling to his feet, Furno took aim with his fire sword. Bursts of flame shot from the blade, melting the speakers one by one. When there was only a single speaker left, the sonic wave stopped. It was replaced by Stringer's voice, saying, "Come in, Furno. It's time we talked."

Furno noticed that the door to the communications tower was wide open. It was an invitation, one he could not afford to turn down.

"Oh, we're going to do more than talk, brain," Furno muttered as he headed for the entrance.

Inside, it was quiet. Furno had half-expected to find a bunch of robots waiting to ambush him, but the place seemed abandoned. At least, it did until a characteristic hum told him his sensors were abruptly working again. Stringer had evidently cut off the jamming signal.

And there he is, Furno thought, looking at the scope, *up on the roof, waiting for me.*

Getting there would mean a long climb up stairs that could be booby-trapped. Furno went back outside and started to climb the outside of the building. It took a while, but when he made it to the top, he saw Stringer's back was to him. *Maybe this will be a short fight after all*, thought Furno.

Stringer suddenly turned and fired a blast from his sonic weapon. Furno ducked down behind the ledge just in time.

"You forget," said Stringer, "I know everything this body knows. Furno would never come up the stairs. So I offered you a tempting target and prepared a proper welcome."

Furno was in trouble and he knew it. Dangling from the ledge, he was vulnerable. All it would take would be one sound wave from Stringer's blaster and he would be falling a long way to the street below. Oddly enough, though, the brain controlling the Hero did not launch an attack.

Cautiously, Furno poked his head up above the edge of the roof. Stringer was just standing there, arms folded, smiling.

"That must be very uncomfortable," said the enslaved Hero. "Why don't you come up here and talk?"

"Um, because you just tried to blast me," Furno replied.

"Oh, that," said Stringer. "I did what you expected me to do. Now that's over and we can talk like civilized beings."

Furno kept a tight grip on his shield and a wary eye on Stringer as he hoisted himself up on the roof. He stood, battle ready, his eyes locked on his opponent. "You want to talk? Let go of my friend."

Stringer laughed. "Actually, that wasn't the topic I had in mind."

"If you expect me to stand still while you put a brain on my head, know that that's not going to—" Furno began.

"No, no," Stringer cut him off. "I admit that was the plan originally. But I've since had a better idea."

"Yeah, I have a few ideas, too," Furno said, raising his sword.

Surprisingly, Stringer made no move to attack. Instead, he said, "Look at me. What do you see?"

"A good friend with a big, ugly brain on his head," Furno shot back.

"Exactly. That is what any of your kind would see. It's an excellent image for inspiring fear and disgust, but not obedience. That is where you come in."

Stringer leaned against a half-crumbled chimney. "If we have to, we can take control of everyone in this galaxy once Hero Factory is destroyed. But it would take time and we have better things to do. But if the robot population could be persuaded that defeat is inevitable, they might follow us without having to be mind controlled. Think of the suffering that would be avoided!"

"Right, for a brain, you're all heart," snapped Furno. "What does this have to do with me?"

"We need a . . . face," answered Stringer. "We need someone who is respected by the robots of this galaxy, and someone we are not controlling directly. It must be someone who will inspire trust and confidence . . . a Hero. Think about it: If you were to tell the robot population to follow our lead, who would dare argue with you? You are the famous Furno!"

A bitter laugh came from Furno's throat. "Wait a minute, you expect me to join up with you? And then I'm supposed to talk everyone into being your slave? You're insane!"

Stringer's expression turned serious. "We are perfect creations. No mental defect is possible. We cannot be 'insane,' as you put it."

"Okay, how about flat on your back?" Furno said, leaping toward Stringer. He crashed into the other robot, knocking him onto the hard surface of the roof.

Stringer lashed out with a kick, but Furno moved just enough that he only received a glancing blow. He grabbed Stringer's wrist and tried to force it down so that the sonic blaster would be pointed away. But Stringer managed to get off a shot, the sound waves shattering the chimney. Bricks rained down on Furno, startling him just enough that Stringer was able to flip him over.

Now it was Furno on the ground and Stringer

standing over him, weapon pointed right at his Hero Core. Furno brought his shield up and struck Stringer's weapon, sending it flying off the roof. Then he used a sweeping kick to bring Stringer down again.

Stringer grabbed on to the blade of Furno's sword, trying to wrestle the weapon away from him. Furno's first thought was to trigger the sword's power and let its flame discourage the brain from trying to steal it. As soon as he thought of the idea, he stopped himself—doing that would injure Stringer's body, and he had to try to avoid that.

With a sharp, wrenching motion, Stringer managed to get the sword away. He aimed it at Furno, but nothing happened. Furno realized that he had not gotten the weapon until after his last adventure with Stringer, so the veteran Hero would not know how to work it. And if he didn't know, the brain controlling him wouldn't know, either.

Furno saw an opportunity. Stringer was holding the sword with both hands. As fast as he could, Furno snatched the Hero cuffs off

Stringer's belt and snapped them on the controlled robot's wrists. Then he brought his hand down in a swift chop, making Stringer drop the sword. Furno scooped it up.

"Fight's over," said Furno. "Get off my friend. Now."

"So that you can use that sword on me?" answered the brain through Stringer's mouth. "We are brains without bodies. We're not stupid."

"I'm a Hero," Furno replied. "We don't kill our enemies. You'll be taken back to Hero Factory as a prisoner and treated well."

Stringer took a step toward the edge of the roof. "I told you the last time we met what I could make this body do — leap to its doom — if I say so. Release me or I'll do it."

"You'd sacrifice yourself because you lost a fight?"

"I haven't lost," Stringer answered. "My army is still out there, about to seize your precious weapons system. My species will still win. But you have dared to oppose us, and I would sacrifice myself to hurt you."

Before Furno could move, Stringer took another step, his foot dangling over the edge of the roof. "No!" yelled Furno, rushing forward.

In the next moment, Stringer was bathed by a beam of light and began to slowly rise into the air. The brain made the Hero look up. "What? Impossible!" Stringer cried.

Furno glanced up as well. There, hovering above the roof and holding Stringer in a tractor beam, was the Hero craft. That was amazing enough, but the fact that no one seemed to be in the cockpit was downright weird.

"Hello?" said Furno into his helmet microphone. "Who's in that ship?"

There was a loud burst of static. Then Furno heard Stormer's voice. "—you hear me? This is Stormer. Can anyone hear me?"

"I can hear you," said Furno. "Stringer was jamming the signals, but that's done for now. Where are you, Stormer?"

The Alpha Team leader explained how he was still at Hero Factory, but controlling the Hero craft remotely. "What's your situation?" asked Stormer.

"Desperate in the extreme," was Furno's answer. "I need Stringer's help to fix things here, but he's not going to volunteer under the circumstances. Request permission to take action."

"What kind of action, Furno?"

"I have to get that brain off his head," the Hero replied, "no matter what the risk."

There was a long pause. Furno could imagine what Stormer was thinking. The team leader and Stringer had been friends a long time. Finally, Stormer said, "I can have Zib and a repair team there in a matter of hours."

Furno glanced off the roof at the mass of enslaved robots moving toward the entrance to the underground complex. "We don't have hours, and neither does the galaxy!"

Reaching up, he grabbed Stringer's ankle and pulled him out of the tractor beam, dropping him to the ground. In a previous encounter with the brains, Hero Factory had learned that their weak spot was where their spiked "tails" connected to the base of the brain. Furno struck that spot, hard, and the brain abruptly detached from Stringer's head. As it tried to attack Furno, the young Hero tossed the creature against the wall, knocking it unconscious.

Furno waited tensely. Although the method worked, it was not without risk. A sudden cutoff of the link to the brain could scramble a robot's programming, and that was the least of the possible side effects.

"Furno! Report!" Stormer broadcast.

"Stringer is free and the brain is . . . asleep," said Furno. "You need to get the Hero craft to Bulk's location as soon as you can. He's going to need it."

"Furno, I'm dispatching all available Heroes to your location," Stormer said. "Sit tight."

"No time to sit tight, sir," said Furno. "Be prepared for another communications blackout in the next few minutes. That will be the signal to move in. Furno out." Stringer moaned and started to sit up.

"What . . . what happened?" said Stringer. "I remember being inside the communications tower, and then . . ."

Furno helped the Hero to his feet, feeling relieved. So far, Stringer wasn't exhibiting any signs of damage from what he had gone through. "That happened," said Furno, pointing at the brain. "And it's going to happen a lot more if you can't help me stop it."

Furno explained his plan as he and Stringer ran down the stairs. "We can't stop the brains," he said. "There are too many of them."

"So what's your idea?"

"A large-scale version of the electromagnetic pulse the new Hero craft can do," said Furno. "If we can rig this communications tower to broadcast a pulse like that, we can shut down every robot in the city. Without the robots, the brains can't do much."

"Won't that shut us down, too?"

"Not if we move fast enough. Can we pull this off?"

Stringer pushed his way through a door and they raced out into the hallway. In a matter of moments, they found what they were looking for—one of the main communications control centers. Stringer looked around at the equipment and frowned.

"It might be possible," he said. "But this tower isn't powerful enough to blanket the whole city. That's why they had more than one, but the rest are wrecked."

"What can we do?"

Stringer crouched down and looked at the wiring below one of the larger control panels. "If we had a satellite that we could bounce the signal off of, something that would be shielded from the pulse itself . . . but where could we get something like that?"

Furno smiled. "I might just have an answer to that."

Bulk hated to admit it, but he was getting

tired. He and Karter had been baiting and bashing brains for quite a while now, but it was a lot like trying to clean a whole Hero craft with one piece of tissue. They could stop some of the controlled robots and divert others, but not all of them.

He was also getting worried that there had been no signal from Furno. If the fiery Hero had failed in his task, then all he and Karter were doing was delaying the inevitable. The brains would get them both in the end.

When he heard the familiar jet engines, Bulk first thought he was imagining things. He was even surer of it when he saw a pilotless Hero craft landing on the street in front of him. Just as it touched down, Furno's voice came over the radio.

"Bulk? Do you read me?"

"I got you, Furno," said Bulk. "You're not going to believe what's right in front of me."

"A Hero craft with no pilot?"

"Wow, you're good," said Bulk. "What's the status?"

"I've got Stringer. He's back on our side."

"Way to go!" said Bulk. "How is he?"

"He's in the same trouble we're in," answered Furno. "Get Karter and take the Hero craft back to the complex. There have to be shielded areas in there. Herd everyone into one of them, but don't seal the door. Stringer and I will be on our way."

"Got it!"

Bulk and Karter got into the Hero craft and took off. Bulk flew low, banking the craft to get a view of the main entrance to the underground lab. What he saw turned his inner mechanisms cold.

"Furno, we've got a problem — a big one," he broadcast. "The main doors to the lab are caved in and there are robots with brains on 'em streaming inside. I think they've taken the complex. I can pick up you and Stringer and we can get off the planet until help gets here."

"You're forgetting Project Sunstorm," said Furno. "If they have the complex, they have the weapons system. They'll blow the Hero craft right out of the sky, along with any others that show up. We need to go ahead with the plan. Get inside and get to safety, however you can!"

"Okay. Just tell Stormer to take the cost of the Hero craft out of my pay," Bulk joked. "Over and out."

"What are you planning?" asked Karter.

"If I knew, I would tell you," answered Bulk.

Back at the communications tower, Stringer and Furno were working hard and working fast. "It's not much," said Stringer. "But it should knock out anything electronic for five or six hours at least. That assumes they don't move the satellites on us, which, from what you said, they can now do whenever they like."

"They don't know they have a reason to," said Furno. "You and Bulk are the only ones who know the plan." He smiled. "And Bulk promised to try and forget it in case he got captured."

"Should I set the timer?"

"Let's wait a minute," said Furno. "We have to

give Bulk a chance to get in the complex."

"What if he doesn't get in?" asked Stringer. "What then?"

"Without a safe refuge from the EM pulse, we'll go down, too," Furno answered. "That would be a disaster. Remember, the robots are being shut down, but the brains will still be active. If we pass out—"

"They can attach themselves to us while we sleep," said Stringer grimly. "Been there, done that, not again. Come on, Bulk, what are you waiting for?"

As it turned out, Bulk was no longer waiting for anything. He had thrown the Hero craft into a power dive, headed right for the camouflaged roof of the complex. Karter wasn't taking this approach well.

"Are you insane? We could go in the way we got out, through the side entrance!"

"That was fine when the enemy wasn't inside

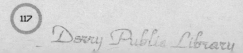

there," Bulk answered, his eyes fixed on the target. "Now we need to shake them up a little."

"Shake them up, or smash us up?"

"Keep quiet," growled Bulk. "I'm driving here."

The ground came up rapidly. To his credit, Karter never shut down his optic sensors. If these were going to be his final moments, he would watch it happen.

The Hero craft plowed into the ground and smashed its way through the reinforced ceiling of the complex. The impact was incredible and Bulk could hear the shriek of metal as the Hero craft's body was ripped and torn by rock and steel. For an impossibly long moment, it looked like the ship would not make it all the way through the barriers and into the complex. Then there was suddenly light before them, as the nose of the craft crashed through the ceiling of the main lab. Rock and dust rained down all around.

Bulk shattered the windshield with one punch, grabbed Karter, and dragged him out of the vehicle. He jumped to the floor amidst the chaos spawned by their arrival.

Trained in combat, Bulk knew how to scan a room for threats in an instant. Here, there were plenty. Dumacc and a dozen security robots all had brains on their heads. Worse, Dumacc was at the console that controlled Project Sunstorm.

"You're too late!" the controlled scientist cried. "We have the weapon!"

"Furno, do it!" Bulk shouted into his helmet mike.

"How—?!" said Dumacc. "We lost all contact with Stringer. We know he must have been captured by Furno. But Sunstorm will eliminate them both."

"You're aiming it at the city?" said Karter, in disbelief. "You'll burn up the whole place!"

Dumacc shook his head, a smile of madness on his face. "The equations have been solved. The process works. We can aim the flare with pinpoint accuracy. And if not . . . well, we will be safe down here."

"Nice," said Bulk. "Hundreds of your own species are up above in that city."

"It doesn't matter how many brains are destroyed," Dumacc replied. "More can always be made."

"Bulk, look at the console!" said Karter. "See those yellow lights flashing?"

"Yeah, what about them?"

"It means Sunstorm is overloading again," Karter replied. "We have to stop him!"

Together, the Hero and the spy waded into the security robots. There was no time to worry about how many blows they took or how many laser blasts just missed them. Like rockets soaring to a distant planet, they kept moving forward, never wavering for their destination.

Watching them come closer and closer, the brain controlling Dumacc became a little frantic. He started trying to rush the Sunstorm process, which only made the warning lights flash more insistently. Now the yellow lights had been joined by red ones.

"Hey, Karter," Bulk said as he elbowed aside

a security robot. "Flashing red lights are a bad thing, I'm guessing?"

"Yeah, Hero," Karter snapped. "Try 'nothing left of the planet' bad."

"Thought so," said Bulk. "Just another day at the office."

"Furno, do it!"

Bulk's voice came over the receivers in the communications tower. Stringer looked at Furno, who nodded. Stringer touched two wires together and then hurried to his feet.

"We've got fifteen minutes until everyone on this planet shuts down," he said. "If we don't want to join them, we better move."

The two Heroes made it out to the street and started to run. Most of the controlled robots were still streaming toward the complex and so not taking much notice of Furno and Stringer. They managed to get to the complex with a couple minutes to spare, only to see a traffic jam of enemy robots trying to get in the main entrance.

"Side door?" asked Stringer.

"We'd have to get past them to reach it," said Furno. "How about we go through the skylight?"

"What skylight?"

Furno pointed at the tail of the Hero craft sticking out of the ground. "The one Bulk made."

Taking care to stay out of sight of the massed robots, the two climbed up the Hero craft and then slid along the side of it and through the hole. They fell to the lab floor in the midst of the pitched battle going on for the control room.

"Any idea what's going on?" Furno said.

"Hit the guys with the brains," Stringer replied.

"Always a good strategy," Furno agreed.

Together, the three Heroes and Karter made short work of the security robots. It was Bulk who seized Dumacc and yanked him away from the console. "Somebody want to shut this machine down?"

Karter took a step toward it, but Bulk blocked his way. "Someone other than the bad guy?" the Hero said.

Stringer was able to master the controls in a few moments and shut it down. But he knew the clock was ticking down to another deadline. "We need to find a safe room!"

Karter led the way to a chamber in the rear of the lab. Just before they entered, Bulk shoved Dumacc aside. "No brains allowed, sorry."

Furno shut the chamber door behind them. A few seconds later, the lights flickered in the lab and then the consoles abruptly went dead. At the same time, every robot that hadn't already been knocked out collapsed to the floor as the electro-magnetic pulse temporarily shut down their systems. Some of the brains were stunned by the fall; others began to detach themselves from their unconscious hosts.

Stringer counted down to himself until he knew the pulse would have stopped. Then he opened the door and stepped out into the lab.

A few of the brains moved toward him, but a blast from Furno's fire sword discouraged them from further progress.

"So it worked?" asked Bulk.

"We can't check the monitors, so we'll have to go look," said Stringer.

Outside of the lab, the complex was eerily quiet. All around were unconscious robots, more and more of them as they approached the main entrance. Confused brains crawled out from the piles of sleepers, trying to find an active robot to take over.

"Good job, you guys," Bulk said to Furno and Stringer.

"It was his idea," said Stringer. "I just crossed the wires."

"Yeah, your wires have been crossed for as long as I've known you," Bulk said, clapping Stringer on the back. "Good to have you back, buddy."

A few hours later, Stormer arrived with Zib,

Breez, Rocka, Evo, Nex, and a dozen other Heroes. They immediately began capturing the brains and readying portable stasis chambers to house them.

"It's going to take years to repair this city," said Stormer. "It's a shame."

"You think the robots will rebuild again?" asked Breez.

Stormer nodded. "It's their home, the same way Hero Factory is ours. So, yes, they will find a way to bring Tranquis back again."

Breez thought about his words. She hadn't been a member of Hero Factory all that long, but she had always thought of the place as headquarters, not home. She guessed that when she had been on the team as long as Stormer, she would consider it the way he did. Somehow, she wasn't looking forward to that.

As the cleanup continued, Bulk was the first to notice someone was missing. "Hey, where's Karter?"

"He was cleaning up rubble near the Hero craft, last I saw," said Evo.

"Aw, no," said Bulk, heading back into the complex.

He found Karter in the main lab. Zib was on the floor, unconscious, and Karter was tearing the wiring out of the Sunstorm device.

"You've got a lot of bad habits," said Bulk. "You really need to break them, before I break you."

"I'm doing you a favor," Karter replied. "You don't want this weapon to fall into the wrong hands, do you?"

"Pal, hands don't get any more 'wrong' than yours," said Bulk.

Karter's hands barely moved, but somehow he suddenly was holding a dagger. He lunged at Bulk, but the Hero dodged and grabbed Karter's wrist.

"Really?" said Bulk. "After all I've been through the last couple days, you really want to go after me with a pointy piece of metal? Watch."

Bulk snatched the dagger out of Karter's hand and crushed it into a tiny ball. Then he let go of Karter and tossed the remains of the weapon to him.

"There, your very own Hero Factory souvenir."

Karter didn't seem at all grateful for the gift.

"Come on, Karter," Bulk said, grabbing him by the arm and starting to escort him from the lab. "We've got enough brains up to no good on this planet. We don't need yours, too."

Epilogue

A week later, Stormer, Zib, Bulk, Stringer, and Furno sat in the briefing room at Hero Factory. The mood was one of relief and worry at the same time.

"How's Tranquis?" asked Bulk.

"Stable, for now," said Stormer. "When the robots went down, a lot of the brains abandoned them. Our teams were able to round them up and put them into stasis. Of the ones that didn't let go, we had to put them and the robot they were attached to into stasis together. We couldn't risk any of those robots waking up and another rampage starting."

"And Sunstorm? What are we doing about that?" asked Furno.

"A most remarkable project," Zib replied, "but incredibly dangerous. Dumacc thought he had solved the problems that caused the environmental disaster on Tranquis, but he had not. In fact, he had made them worse. Karter was right—if they had tried to use the weapon again, the entire planet would have been incinerated. It's been dismantled, and Rocka and Evo are preparing a report on its workings."

"Then we're good?" said Bulk.

"No," Stormer said sharply, rising from the table. "We're far from good. This is our third encounter with the brains and we still know almost nothing about them: What are they? Who created them? Where are they from, and why are they targeting our galaxy?

"On top of that, we have a conspiracy among the frontier worlds to build a superweapon," he continued. "What were they going to do with it? Was it purely for defense, or could they have taken aggressive action against other regions with it?"

"I can answer the last part," said Zib. "If they had launched more satellites to relay the flare, they could have hit anywhere in the galaxy. The satellites themselves had unstable cores—they were designed that way so that if they were attacked, they would explode so violently they could wipe out half a fleet. Clever, but in a terrible sort of way . . ."

"Karter won't talk," said Stringer. "We know someone planned and paid for all that research and equipment, but we still don't know who—or if they had any connection to the brains."

"So we didn't win," said Furno. "We just survived."

Bulk shook his head. "Nah, don't think like that. We saved a whole lot of robots and stopped the brains and whoever these other bad guys are from getting their hands on a really nasty weapon. That's a win, in my book."

"In mine, too," said Stormer. "But it's not enough. We can't just be on our guard against these brains anymore, because they are striking too fast and too unpredictably. We need to take the fight to them somehow."

Furno turned to Stringer. "Is there anything you can remember? Anything that might help?"

Stringer looked down at the table, concentrating, trying to recall something of his experience. After a few minutes, he said, "It's not them. . . ."

"What do you mean?" asked Zib.

"All of this, it wasn't their idea," Stringer replied. "The brains are a weapon, no different from Sunstorm. Someone is using them, aiming them right at us. Whoever that is, they're the real enemy."

"Brains. Brain-makers. Conspirators. We sure have a lot of folks out to get us," said Bulk. "It's enough to make you feel unloved."

"I want answers," Stormer said to the group. "Find some. Dismissed."

Zib and the Heroes filed out, all but Stringer. "You're scared," he said to Stormer.

"We're fighting shadows," the Alpha Team leader replied. "So far, we've been lucky. One day, our luck will run out, and then what happens? Of course I'm scared."

"What are you thinking?"

Stormer turned his back on his friend and stared at the monitor screen. It showed a huge image of one of the brains. "That maybe our day is past. Maybe the threats we face now are too big even for Hero Factory. I mean, look at Project Sunstorm — it was created by the robots we're here to protect. Meanwhile, they're plotting behind our backs!"

"Did you ever stop to think maybe they're scared, too?"

Stormer turned to look at his old friend. "What are you talking about?"

"All too often, we're all that stands between them and menaces like the Witch Doctor or Von Nebula or Black Phantom," said Stringer. "A team of robots with our Hero craft going up against the worst the galaxy has to offer — and sometimes, it must seem like a pretty thin line of defense. Can we really blame them if they start trying to find ways to defend themselves?"

Stringer expected Stormer to argue with him, but the Alpha Team leader just nodded and said, "We're no longer effective. We're no longer enough. Is that what you think?"

"I don't know," Stringer said, shrugging. "I do believe the menaces are getting bigger and more powerful, and we're staying the same. Sure, we can upgrade armor and weapons and train new Heroes, but we're still fighting crime the way we have since the old days. It's a new era, and maybe it needs new methods."

Stormer hit a button and the screen changed. Now it showed a chemical formula Stringer wasn't familiar with. He peered at it and then took a step back, startled by what it seemed to be.

"Is that—?" he began.

"Yes," said Stormer. "Zib gave it to me yesterday. It's a model for a whole new source of power for everything from Hero Cores to Hero craft. If it works . . . well, there won't be much we can't do, Stringer."

Stringer said nothing for a long time. It was Stormer who broke the silence, saying, "The conspiracy will have to wait. We need to find out who created the brains and why. Then we put a stop to them."

Stormer walked out of the room, leaving Stringer to gaze at the screen. Something about the formula he saw gave him a bad feeling. One way or the other, he knew, everything about Hero Factory was on the verge of changing forever. . . .

Bulk caught up with Furno on his way to the gym. "Hey, Furno, why the rush?"

"Stormer's right," said Furno. "We have to be ready, and more than ready. The brains will be back again."

Bulk put a hand on Furno's shoulder. "Hey . . . you did really good today. Without you, there'd be no more Tranquis . . . or Stringer."

"I know," said Furno, shaking him off. "But the job isn't done."

"What job ever is?" said Bulk. "If you stop a river from flooding, you think it's never going to rain again? If you stop a volcano from erupting, is that it, never again? We can't end evil, Furno . . . just stop it in its tracks."

"And what if we can't?" said Furno. "What if there are too many of them, and too few of us?"

"We're Hero Factory," said Bulk. "We find a way."

Karter sat in a cell in Hero Factory's recently rebuilt prison. He was awaiting trial on a whole host of charges and would probably end up spending several years in jail. Of course, he could have made a deal by sharing all he knew with the Heroes, but that wasn't how he did business.

Besides, he had no intention of ever going to trial.

The Heroes who had searched him had been thorough, but Karter's employers had tech they had never heard of here. When he was certain no guards were close enough to hear him, he gently slid one fingertip to the right, exposing a sophisticated communication device.

"This is Karter," he whispered. "Are you receiving?"

"We are," came the response. "Why are you contacting us, Karter? You failed in your mission and allowed yourself to be captured."

"No, I created a situation where I was able to infiltrate Hero Factory," Karter hissed. "I showed initiative while you hid in the dark, afraid they might find out you exist."

"Make your report," was the icy reply.

"Hero Factory knows about the conspiracy now," Karter said.

"Due to your bungling?"

"More Dumacc having nerves like water," said Karter. "They are occupied with these brains, or whatever those disgusting creatures really are, but when that's done . . . they are going to come for you."

This time there was no anger in the voice that answered, just worry. "Why? All we are trying to do is protect ourselves."

Karter gave a harsh laugh. "Right. Maybe you

can fool some of your lab techs with that, but not Stormer and his crew. You can't build super-weapons on their watch and get away with it, friend."

"Then what do you recommend?"

Karter smiled a thin smile. "Well, you're always complaining that they aren't effective or necessary . . . so why not simply destroy them? With Hero Factory out of the way, you can build whatever weapons you like . . . and 'protect' the whole galaxy if you want . . . and who is going to tell you no?"

There was silence on the other end of the line. Karter knew his employers were thinking about it. When they spoke again, it was simply to say, "You can do this?"

"I can arrange for it to be done," Karter assured them.

"Then do it." The line went dead.

Karter leaned back and sighed. *This has been a good day*, he thought. *Hopefully, it will be the first of many . . . but not for Hero Factory. Oh no.*

Hero Factory has very, very *few days left.*